HOW I BECAME A SUPERHERO

Don't miss this other nail-biting **MAXimum Boy** adventure:
THE DAY EVERYTHING TASTED LIKE BROCCOLI

MAXimum Boy

starring in
HOW I BECAME A SUPERHERO

Originally titled: The Hijacking of Manhattan

BY DAN GREENBURG
ILLUSTRATIONS BY GREG SWEARINGEN

A Little Apple Paperback

SCHOLASTIC
New York   Toronto   London   Auckland   Sydney
Mexico City   New Delhi   Hong Kong

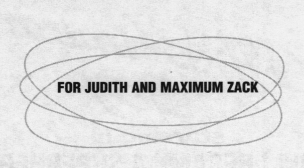

FOR JUDITH AND MAXIMUM ZACK

ISBN 0-439-21944-2

Text copyright © 2001 by Dan Greenburg
Illustration copyright © 2001 by Scholastic Inc.

12 11 10 9 8 7 6 5 4 3 2 1   1 2 3 4 5 6/0

Printed in the U.S.A.
First Scholastic printing, May 2001

CHAPTER 1

They call me Maximum Boy. It's a stupid name, I know, but they started calling me that in the newspapers. And now it's on my costume, so I'm stuck with it.

My real name is Max Silver. It all started about three years ago when I was eight. I was in the Air and Space Museum in Washington, D.C., on a class trip. I was watching a guy set up an exhibit of rocks they'd just brought back from space. The rocks were blue and glowing. The guy handling the rocks was wearing a space suit and space gloves. He was standing on a rickety stepladder. He sneezed: "Ah . . . ah . . . ah . . . ah-CHOOOFFF!" He lost his balance and dropped the space rocks. I caught them.

"Drop them! Drop those rocks!" he screamed. "Ah-CHOOOFFF!"

"Why?" I asked. Usually when you catch somebody's space rocks what they say is "Thanks!"

"Because. They're dangerous! Ah-CHOOOFFF! They're radioactive!"

So I dropped them. But it was too late. Handling them just that little bit did something to me. The head of the Air and Space Museum insisted I go see a doctor the second

I got back home to Chicago. "I'll pay for it myself," he said.

The doctor examined me. He told my parents there was absolutely nothing wrong with me. OK, I do glow a tiny bit in the dark. Otherwise, I look like any other eleven-year-old boy with glasses and braces. But I can do stuff that most eleven-year-old boys can't. Like fly. And run faster than trains. And lift eighteen-wheel tractor-trailers over my head with one hand. And blow soap bubbles out of my nose.

I do have a few weaknesses: hayfever — ragweed makes me sneeze my head off; milk products — I get a bad upset stomach whenever I eat them; and math, of course. It's not just that I'm not good at math, it's that even *seeing* a math problem makes me weak and dizzy. I'm probably the only kid who has a doctor's excuse to get out of math.

Anyway, when I found out how strong I was, I didn't want anybody to know. I guess I was embarrassed. Then, a few weeks after handling the space rocks, something happened that changed everything.

I was walking in Grant Park near my parents' apartment. People ride horses in Grant Park. It's a great park that runs along the shore of Lake Michigan. Anyway, this particular day, a horse fell into a ditch. It hurt its leg and the lady who was riding him was trapped underneath. I lifted the horse out of the ditch. I checked to make sure the horse and the lady were OK. They were. Then I ran away.

The lady was grateful. She told the

newspapers what I did. Everybody got all excited. Big deal.

I did some other stuff. Flew to the top of a tall tree to rescue a kitten. Caught some muggers. Caught a refrigerator that fell out of a window before it squashed an old man. Threw myself in front of a bus before it hit a little kid. Blah, blah, blah. I liked helping out, but I didn't like all the fuss and attention. I started carrying a mask, so if I had to help somebody out I could slip it on and no one would know who I was.

As I said before, the newspapers began calling me Maximum Boy and the name stuck. My mom made me a costume: a black mask; a black baseball shirt with Maximum Boy spelled out in script; a black baseball cap with the letters MB on the front; black baseball pants; black cleats; and a cape (which is a little embarrassing, but I've got to admit it helps when I fly). Oh, yeah, the cape is silver. Like I said, my name is Max Silver, so I guess that's where Mom got the color.

Unless I use my superpowers, I'm a really lousy athlete. Before I got my superpowers I was either the slowest kid in class or the second slowest, depending on whether Roland Shlotzky was in school that day. When we pick teams to play baseball, football, basketball, or soccer, I'm always the last kid to be chosen. Sometimes they actually fight over me. "We got Shlotzky, so you gotta take Silver," they'll say.

It's pretty humiliating. It's also pretty stupid. I mean, with my superpowers, I'm about a thousand times faster and stronger than any kid in my school. But if I used my superpowers, I'd blow my cover, so I can't do that. I once thought I could use just a *little* of my superpowers, but that's not the way it works with superpowers. It's either all or nothing. So I have to put up with a lot of jerks in gym telling me how much I stink at sports.

Our gym teacher, Mrs. Hunkenhoffer, is built like Arnold Schwarzenegger. Because I'm such a lousy athlete she has no respect for me. In fact, I think she hates me. I wonder how she'd treat me if she knew I was Maximum Boy. Probably a whole lot differently.

Besides me, only seven people know I'm Maximum Boy: (1) my mom, Rose; (2) my dad, Sam; (3) my teenage sister, Tiffany; (4) my best friend, Charlie Sparks; (5) my teacher, Mrs. Mulvahill; (6) our family doctor,

Dr. Warren; (7) the President of the United States.

The President is always calling me to help him out whenever stuff happens that he can't handle. Like that day last December.

At four A.M., the island of Manhattan started moving away from the other four boroughs of New York City. The people of Manhattan were pretty annoyed.

Powerful motors were heard up near the north end. Then the island of Manhattan began moving away. Staten Island was shoved aside. Manhattan started slowly chugging out to sea.

Loudspeakers had been hung from lampposts. A voice over the loudspeakers said Manhattan was being stolen. It was a foggy day. Soon Manhattan completely disappeared in the heavy mist.

We first heard about all this on TV at breakfast. It was a Wednesday.

"Oh, Max," said my mom. "I do hope they don't ask you to go to New York now and take care of this."

"Mom," I said, "we live in Chicago. I'm sure they can get somebody on the East Coast to handle it."

"But you know the President is always asking you to do things for him. Like that time he sent you to Indianapolis. Or that time he sent you to outer space."

Right about then our phone rang. Mom answered. She talked for a while, and then she hung up. She looked worried.

"Max, that was the President," she said. "He's just received a ransom note for Manhattan. He wants you to fly to Washington, D.C., right away to help. I told him you have a big geography test this morning, but he said he'd call your teacher and work it out with her."

My sister, Tiffany, got really upset. "How come *Max* gets to miss school all the time, and I *never* do?" she said.

"Max can't help it if he has these super-powers, dear," said my mom. "He touched those space rocks and something strange happened to him. It's like that time you touched those leaves and got poison ivy. Remember?"

"I am so bummed out from hearing all this superhero stuff," said Tiffany. "It's not fair that the President calls Max and gets him excused from *school*."

"Max helps the President with things from time to time. And sometimes he gets excused from school. If you help the President, Tiffany, I'm sure you'll be excused from school, too."

"Thanks a lot," said Tiffany.

"Now, Max," said Mom. "Your Maximum Boy costume is still in the dirty clothes hamper. It has that spaghetti sauce stain on it, and I haven't done the laundry yet."

"That's OK, Mom," I said. "I'm sure the President doesn't care about spaghetti sauce stains."

CHAPTER 2

By the time I got to Washington, the citynapping was on the front page of every newspaper in town.

MANHATTAN MISSING! shouted the headlines. BIG APPLE PLUCKED! NEW YORK CITY VANISHES IN FOG! THIEVES ASK A TRILLION FOR MANHATTAN'S RETURN!

I landed on the South Lawn of the White

House. Two uniformed guards with rifles came over to me. They were Marines.

"Can I help you?" one of the Marines asked me.

"I'm Maximum Boy," I said. "I believe the President is expecting me."

They both saluted me. I got a kick out of that.

"*Sir*, yes, *sir!*" said the Marine who'd asked if he could help me. "Right this way, sir."

The Marines escorted me to the special secret basement entrance at the back of the White House. A member of the Secret Service with something that looked like a hearing aid in his ear spoke into the lapel of his suit jacket.

"Maximum Boy has arrived," he said to his lapel. "Very well, sir."

The President met me in the Oval Office. He was smiling and frowning at the same time.

"Thanks for getting here so quickly, Maximum Boy," said the President. "Did you have any trouble on the way?"

"Oh, there was some heavy air traffic over Ohio, sir," I said. "But then I picked up a strong tailwind and made up the time."

"Good," he said. "How's your mom and dad and your sister, Tiffany?"

"They're fine, sir."

"Great. Be sure and give them my best when you see them next. Here's the ransom note."

He handed me a piece of paper. It was lettered with a red crayon in big capital letters. It said: WE'VE GOT MANHATTAN. IF YOU EVER WANT TO SEE THE BIG APPLE AGAIN, LEAVE

ONE TRILLION DOLLARS IN SMALL BILLS AT THE BASE OF THE SOUTH POLE.

I handed it back to him.

"What should we do, sir?" I asked.

"Well, we don't have much choice," the President said. "For now, we have to play the citynappers' game."

"What game are they playing, sir?" I asked. "I happen to be pretty good at games

— except for sports, I mean. If it's a board game like Scrabble or Boggle, I ought to be able to really kick their butts."

"No, I mean they're playing some kind of game with the citynapping," said the President. "Unless we outsmart them, Manhattan could end up anywhere. We certainly can't afford to lose Manhattan, now can we?"

"A lot of people would miss it, sir," I said. "Well, at least a few of them would."

"Right," said the President. "Then let's go down to the White House garage. There's somebody down there I'd like you to meet."

The President took me down to the garage in the White House basement. We went in his own private presidential elevator. It made a soft, humming sound as it descended. It had knotty pine walls and a minibar. If anybody wanted a drink on the way down to the White House basement, they wouldn't have to wait.

Parked alongside the President's limousine in the White House garage was an armored truck. It looked really strong and safe. Standing next to the armored truck was a man in a black suit and white crew cut. He was frowning even harder than the President.

"Maximum Boy," said the President, "I'd like you to meet the head of the FBI, J. Edgar Poopington."

"It's a pleasure to meet you, sir," I said.

Poopington stuck out his hand. I shook it. It was huge, rough, and dry.

"Glad to have you aboard, Maximum

Boy," he said. "I don't think I need to tell you how serious this case is, do I?"

"No, sir, you don't."

"Good. We're grateful for any help you can give us."

"I'll be glad to do whatever I can, sir."

"Good lad. Is that a blood stain on your costume?"

"No, sir. It's spaghetti sauce."

"Right," said Poopington. "My people at the FBI tell me that a little club soda will take that out for you."

"Thank you, sir."

"If that doesn't work," said the President, "before you put it in the washer you can Shout it out."

"You mean just scream at the stain, sir?" I asked.

"No, no," said the President. "Shout is a stain remover you use in the laundry."

"Oh, right," I said. "I've seen the commercial on TV. I'll tell my mom, sir."

"All right, Maximum Boy," said Poopington. "In this truck here is what the thieves demanded. One trillion dollars in small bills. We'd like you to take it to the South Pole as soon as possible. When you get there, we expect the citynappers will give you further instructions. But don't worry. We have a little surprise cooked up for them."

"What is it?" I asked.

"That's a surprise," said Poopington. "If I told you, it wouldn't be a surprise now, would it?"

"I guess not, sir," I said.

"All right then, Maximum Boy, when can you leave?" Poopington asked.

"As soon as possible, sir. As soon as I go back to Chicago and get permission from my mom and dad."

Poopington looked at the President, rolled his eyes, then turned back to me.

"How are you planning to transport the armored truck to the South Pole, Maximum Boy?" he asked.

"In the usual way, sir," I said. "I plan to carry it with me as I fly."

By the time I got back to Chicago it was late afternoon. My mom was in the kitchen, cooking dinner. Dad was in the living room, reading his newspaper. My sister, Tiffany, was putting glitter on her long black finger-nails. She hardly looked up when I came in.

"So, *Minimum* Boy, how is the *President?*" she asked.

"Oh, he's OK," I said.

"And what little *favor* does he want you to do for him this time?"

"Oh, nothing much," I answered. "He just wants me to take an armored truck filled with a trillion dollars to the South Pole."

"Oh, yeah?" she said. "So where'd you put this armored truck of his?"

"I left it in front of our building," I said.

Tiffany looked up from painting her nails.

"You left a trillion dollars of the President's money out on the *street*? Mom!" she screamed. "Listen to what Max did!"

Mom hurried in from the kitchen.

"What's all the fuss about?" she asked.

"Mom, the President gave Max an ar-

mored truck with a trillion dollars in it to take to the South Pole. *Minimum* Boy left it in the street."

"Max," said Mom. "Did you leave a truck with a trillion dollars out on the street?"

"It's OK, Mom," I said. "I locked the doors and rolled up the windows."

"Well, if you're sure it's safe," said my mom. She started to go back into the kitchen.

"That's *it*?" said Tiffany. "Max leaves a trillion dollars out on the street, and you're OK with it? I leave eight dollars on top of the car and I'm a deranged *maniac*."

"Now, Tiffany," said Mom. "I certainly don't think you're a deranged maniac. Max left the money *inside* the car. You left it on *top* of the car. But you're absolutely right, dear. If it's wrong for you, it's wrong for Max, too."

Dad came into the room, folding his newspaper.

"So, Max, how was the President?" he asked.

"Pretty good," I said. "He said to give you his best."

"Oh, that's nice," said my mom. "I didn't vote for him, but he seems like a polite man."

"So what does he want you to do for him this time?" asked my dad.

"Take an armored truck with a trillion dollars in it to the South Pole," I said.

"Dad, Max left the truck with the trillion dollars right out on the *street*," said Tiffany. "Mom said it was fine. Mom said, 'Anytime you have a truck with a trillion dollars in it, Max, leave it right out on the street.'"

"I *did not* say it was fine, Tiffany," said Mom. "That is most certainly *not* what I said."

"Dad, Tiffany is just jealous because she thinks I'm getting special treatment," I said.

"Which you *are*," said Tiffany. "If *I'd* left that truck out on the street, Mom would ground me for forty *years*!"

"What did you *expect* me to do with that truck, Tiffany?" I asked. "Bring it up to the apartment? Put it in your room?"

"Not the whole truck," said Tiffany. "Just the money!"

"Just the money?" I said. "A trillion dollars in small bills? Do you have any idea how much room that would take up? It would fill up the entire living room!"

"Enough!" yelled my dad. "Can't you two just give it a rest?"

"I'm sorry, Dad," I said.

"Sorry, Dad," said Tiffany.

Dad frowned at us for a couple of seconds, then he relaxed.

"So," said Dad, "when are you leaving for the South Pole, son?"

"As soon as I eat my dinner."

"It's very cold at the Pole, Max," said my mom. "I want you to take your earmuffs and your warm mittens."

"Mom, I won't be *cold*," I said. "I have superpowers, OK?"

"Excuse *me*," said my mom. "You may have superpowers, young man, but I'm still your mother, and I still worry about you. You don't have to bite my head off."

"I'm really sorry, Mom," I said. "I certainly didn't mean to bite your head off."

"Max, if you have time before you leave," said my dad, "I'd appreciate your help on something."

"What's that?"

"One of the tires on the car is flat. Our jack doesn't work, so I want you to pick up the car while I change the tire. It shouldn't take more than five or ten minutes — tops."

"Dad, I promised the President I'd get that armored truck down to the Pole right away. Can't I do the car tomorrow?"

"I suppose so," said Dad. "Hey, do you at least have a minute for a little arm wrestling? I bet I can beat you this time."

I've arm wrestled my dad 487 times. I've beaten him 485 of those times. The other two I let him win. I thought it might be good for him.

"We can arm wrestle when I get back, Dad," I said. "I'm in kind of a hurry now."

"OK."

"Now, Max," said my mom. "I hope you're not planning to fly faster than a thousand miles per hour. Especially at night. I don't want you sideswiping any jumbo jets."

"Mom, if I don't fly faster than a thousand miles per hour, it'll take *forever* to get there. I might not even get back by bedtime."

"You'd *better* get back by bedtime, Max," said my mom. "Otherwise you won't be allowed any more missions on school nights. And remember, when you come back, you still have homework to do."

"What's the latest I can be back?" I asked.

"Bedtime on school nights is nine-thirty *sharp*."

"But, Mom. What if I'm in the middle of a fight with international criminals?"

"Tell them your mother says bedtime is nine-thirty sharp. They'll understand. International criminals have mothers, too. Will you at least promise me you won't fly any faster than the speed of light? Albert Einstein says things disintegrate if they go faster than the speed of light."

"OK, Mom, I promise," I said.

CHAPTER 3

When I got down to Antarctica it was completely white. There was nothing but ice and snow and glaciers in all directions. It didn't look like night, but it didn't look like day, either. The sky just kind of glowed.

I couldn't see a single living thing in any direction. Not even a penguin or a polar bear.

The wind whistled. The glaciers made

creepy, cracking noises. It was pretty cold. The thermometer on my wristwatch read 140 degrees below zero. My fingers and toes were completely numb. I wished I'd taken the earmuffs and mittens, but I'll never admit that to my mom.

Off in the distance I spotted it. The South Pole. A green-and-white-striped pole about thirty feet high, with a red flag on top of it. I set the armored car down gently on the ice. At the base of the pole was an envelope. It had two words printed on the outside: MAXIMUM BOY.

I tore open the envelope, pulled out the letter inside, and began reading out loud: "Pat is four years older than Bob. Bob is two years older than Jill. Jill is three years older than Jim. How much younger than Pat is Jim?"

I began to feel weak and dizzy. I hadn't realized till it was too late — I'd been reading a math problem!

I staggered backward and fell. What an idiot I'd been to read something out loud without checking what it was first! Well, the citynappers certainly knew my weaknesses. They'd done their homework. I wish they'd done *mine* while they were at it.

It had been a long time since I'd seen a math problem. I forgot how many minutes it took before the effects wore off. All I could do till then was lie helpless in the snow.

Lying helpless in the snow, I heard a team of huskies coming toward me. The dogsled skidded to a stop about a yard from my head. I felt a shower of ice particles on my face as it stopped. Two people jumped off the back of the sled.

One was a giant. He had a bushy red beard and he walked with a limp. The other was very short. He had a big head, a wide duck's bill, a round body covered with fur, human hands, and large webbed feet. He looked like a huge duck-billed platypus.

"So!" said the one who looked like a platypus. "This must be the famous Maximum Boy. At last we meet. Permit me to introduce myself. I am — "

"You're Dr. Cubic Zirkon," I said, "the evil scientist who turned into a duck-billed platypus when an experiment he was doing went terribly wrong."

He cackled with delight.

"Smart boy!" he said. "And this, of course, is my assistant, Nobblock."

"Nobblock," I said. "The crazed serial

killer and former wrestler you helped escape from prison. He once bit the head off an alligator and swallowed it whole."

"I am so glad to see you know who we are," said Dr. Zirkon. "And I am even gladder that you have brought us the ransom. I see you are staring at my feet."

"No, not really."

"Yes, you are," he said. "Don't fib. You are staring at my feet. Have you never seen webbed feet before?"

"Oh, sure," I said. "Lots of times."

"Is that so?" said Dr. Zirkon. "Well, I doubt it. You may think me a freak, Maximum Boy, but I am human, the same as you. I feel joy, the same as you. I feel pain, the same as you. I do everything the same as you. Just with webbed feet, fur, and a duck's bill. Nobblock!"

"Yes, master?"

"Go and count the money."

"In a minute, master."

"*Now*, Nobblock!"

"*OK*, master, *OK*."

"And you," he said to me, "stop staring at my feet."

Nobblock hobbled over to the armored truck. He smashed the back door open with his fist. Then he took out a handful of money. He looked closely at the bills and began to swear.

"Nobblock, what is it?" called Dr. Zirkon.

"The money, master. Take a look."

Dr. Zirkon waddled over to the armored truck. He grabbed a fistful of bills and looked closely at them. Then he roared and threw them into the air. He wheeled and screamed at me.

"Curse you, Maximum Boy!" screamed Dr. Zirkon.

"What's wrong?" I said. "Isn't the armored truck filled with money?"

"It's filled with money, all right," he snorted. "*Monopoly* money!"

Monopoly money! So *this* was the little surprise that Poopington spoke about. I sure wish he had let me in on the fun.

"I had no idea the money was fake, Dr. Zirkon," I said. "I'm just the messenger."

"Is that so?" said Dr. Zirkon. "Well, in this part of the world, we *kill* the messenger! Nobblock?"

Nobblock stepped forward and slugged me. Everything turned black.

CHAPTER 4

I woke up in a creepy room. It was cold and clammy. The walls, ceiling, and floor were made of stone. Cold, filthy, slimy stone. My wrists were fastened to the wall with heavy chains.

Well, heavy chains are not a problem for me. I snap heavy chains like toothpicks. I tugged at the chains on my wrists. They didn't snap like toothpicks, they held like heavy chains. What the heck was going on here?

On the wall facing me was a huge sign. It was so dark I could barely read it. I turned on the infrared vision I use for seeing in the dark and looked again. Now I could read the sign. It said: FRED CAN PAINT A HOUSE IN EIGHT HOURS. BILL CAN PAINT A HOUSE IN NINE HOURS. HOW LONG WILL IT TAKE FRED AND BILL TO PAINT THE HOUSE TOGETHER?

Oh, no! Another math problem! I'd fallen for it again!

I felt like I was going to pass out. I got so weak and dizzy that I would have fallen to the ground if my wrists hadn't been chained to the wall. Just then the door opened. Dr. Zirkon waddled into the room.

"So, Maximum Boy," said the evil platypus. "I do hope you're enjoying your guest room. It is our very best one."

"Yeah," I said. "It's really comfy." I didn't really think it was comfy. I was being sarcastic. But Dr. Zirkon seemed pleased.

"Excellent," he said. "I see you are staring at my beak."

"I'm not staring at your beak," I said. "I have no interest in your stupid beak."

"You think my beak is stupid, do you?" said Dr. Zirkon. He looked pretty upset. "Are you perhaps an expert on beaks, young man? Did you perhaps study beaks in college?"

"No, I didn't," I said.

"Then on what do you base your opinion that my beak is stupid?" he asked.

"Look, I think your beak is fine," I said. "I just happen to be in a bad mood is all."

"I see," he said. Dr. Zirkon crossed his arms and looked at me. He tapped his foot on the stone floor.

"Well," he said, "I'm *waiting*."

"Excuse me?"

"I didn't hear you say you were sorry."

Oh, boy. He wasn't going to let go of this.

"I'm sorry," I said. "I didn't mean it. I apologize for calling your beak stupid, OK?"

Dr. Zirkon laughed a nasty laugh.

"Apology *not* accepted," he said. "Well, Maximum Boy, whether you think my beak is stupid or not, Nobblock and I must leave you now. We must fly up to North America. We shall either collect one trillion *real* dollars from the President of the United States, or else we shall keep the island of Manhattan for ourselves. To make sure you aren't lonely while we're gone, I'm leaving you a little pet."

"A pet?" I said. "What kind of a pet? A cat or a dog, you mean?"

All I needed now was the responsibility of feeding a cat or a dog.

"Oh, no," said Dr. Zirkon. "Neither a cat nor a dog."

He pushed a button behind him. A steel wall slid upward. And then the biggest snake I've ever seen in my life slithered out.

"This," said Dr. Zirkon, "is a giant python, thirty feet long. His name is Horst. Since Horst has not been fed in seven months, he's really looking forward to tonight's dinner. Horst only eats things that are alive. He can swallow a goat or a hundred-pound pig. Or an eleven-year-old boy. How old are you, Maximum Boy?"

"That's for me to know and you to find out," I said. It was a dumb thing to say, but I couldn't think of anything better. Staring at thirty-foot pythons while I'm chained to a wall does that to me sometimes.

"Shall I tell you how death will come?" asked Dr. Zirkon.

"Talk all you want," I said. "I'm not listening."

"Horst will wrap his coils around you and squeeze the breath out of you. Then he will swallow you, headfirst. After you're pulled down into his stomach, he'll start digesting you. That could take up to two weeks. I do hope you don't have anything else planned for the next two weeks?"

"I don't know," I said. "I'll have to check my calendar."

Dr. Zirkon laughed his crazy laugh.

"Check your calendar, eh? That is a good one, Maximum Boy. You are a very funny fellow. Soon you will be a very funny *dead* fellow."

Dr. Zirkon left the cell. The heavy iron door clanked shut behind him.

Horst eyed me with his unblinking stare. Then he slowly slithered toward me. His jaws opened really wide. I could see a long way down his throat.

I felt my strength gradually coming back. But as hard as I tried, I couldn't stop looking at that math problem on the wall. Every time I saw it, I started getting weak and dizzy again.

I closed my eyes. But because of my X-ray vision, I could still see the math problem through my eyelids: FRED CAN PAINT A HOUSE IN EIGHT HOURS. . . .

The snake suddenly coiled itself around me and began to squeeze. It was very hard to inhale. *Don't think about the math problem*, I told myself. *Think about something else. Think about baseball . . . Wrigley Field on opening day . . . the Cubs against the Braves, tie score . . . the Cubs with bases loaded in the bottom of the ninth . . .*

The snake's jaws swallowed up my head. I could feel the pressure on my skull. It was impossible to breathe. I was slowly suffocating. If I didn't breathe soon, I would die.

The math problem on the wall began to fade. My strength started coming back. Just before I blacked out completely, I pulled my head out of the snake's mouth.

I took a deep breath. I wiped the slime off my face. Then, making sure I was facing away from the math problem, I ripped the chains out of the wall. I wrestled the snake off me.

Horst seemed pretty surprised. I guess he was disappointed to miss out on dinner after waiting seven months.

Before I left I twisted him into a big knot.

CHAPTER 5

By the time I took off from Antarctica it was 9:45 P.M. I knew my parents would be really mad I was so late. I flew ten thousand miles per hour all the way back to Chicago.

"Thank heavens you're safe!" my mom said when I got back. She gave me a big hug. "But do you know what time it is?"

"Late, huh?" I said.

"Late? It's nearly eleven P.M. Almost an

hour and a half past your bedtime. And you haven't even done your homework."

"But, Mom, Dr. Zirkon chained me to the wall and a giant python named Horst swallowed my head."

"Well, it's always something, isn't it?" she said. "Have you had anything to eat yet?"

"Not yet," I said.

"Well, then, get washed up while I bring you some dinner. And take off that costume, Max. I need to get out that spaghetti sauce stain."

"I'm not hungry enough for a whole dinner," I said. "Can we skip the veggies?"

"Skip the veggies?" she said. "It's the veggies that keep you strong, Max."

"No, Mom, it's not the veggies. It's the space rocks. Besides, how much stronger could I be? I can already lift an eighteen-wheeler over my head with one hand."

"With veggies you could lift a *twenty*-wheeler," she said.

When I went to school the next morning I was still pretty worried. Either Dr. Zirkon was going to get the trillion dollars from the President, or else he was going to keep Manhattan. There was nothing I could do but wait. My deal with the President is that he calls me only when he needs me. I'm not supposed to call him.

At morning recess, this stupid kid named Trevor Fartmeister came over to me. He's a big kid, about a hundred and eighty pounds. He's in the sixth grade, same as me, but he flunked a couple of times, so he must be around thirteen. Trevor is definitely a bully. Even though he's got a stupid name,

I've never heard anybody make a joke about it. He's got a red buzz cut and half of his left ear is missing. I heard a kid even bigger than Trevor bit it off in a fight. I heard Trevor bit off the other kid's nose.

"Hey, Silver," said Trevor. "How come I didn't see you at recess yesterday?"

"I had to go somewhere," I said.

"Where?"

"To . . . the orthodontist," I said. "There was something wrong with my braces."

"There's a whole lot more wrong with you than your braces, Silver," said Trevor.

He came up really close to me. So close I could see the fillings in his teeth.

"You're such a creep, Silver, I can't even stand to look at you," he said.

"Then don't look at me," I said.

He pushed me hard. I landed on my butt.

"Look at Silver," he yelled to the kids on the playground. "The clumsy klutz tripped over his own feet!"

"Why don't you pick on someone your own size?" said Charlie Sparks.

Charlie is a girl. She's real little, but she isn't afraid of anybody. She happens to be my best friend.

"Why don't you mind your own business?" said Trevor. "Unless you want a piece of me?"

"I don't want any *part* of you," said Charlie.

Trevor laughed and walked away. I picked myself up off the ground.

"Why do you let that big jerk treat you like that?" asked Charlie. "You know you could crush him like a cockroach if you wanted to."

"Sssshhh," I said. "I know that, Charlie. And I'd love to crush him. But that would blow my cover. And I can't let that happen."

"Why not?"

"Because. If everybody knew I was Maximum Boy," I whispered, "bad guys would always be trying to kidnap me and force me to do stuff for them. They might even kidnap my family and hurt them unless I did what they said. It would be a real mess."

Charlie sighed. "I guess you're right."

"The President thinks I'm taking a big risk even with the disguise. He's told me lots of times he wants me to come and live in the White House basement."

"Oh, that would be so cool!" said Charlie.

"No it wouldn't. I'd never be able to go

anywhere or do anything with my family or my friends. It would be like I was in the Witness Protection Program or something. All I could do between missions is sit in the basement, eat pizza, and play video games."

"So what's wrong with that?" she asked.

"Oh, it'd be fun for a while, but then it would be kind of a drag," I said.

"Yeah, I guess you're right. Speaking of the White House," said Charlie much too loudly, "what happened there yesterday?"

"Ssssshhh," I said, looking around to make sure nobody heard her. Sometimes I wonder if I made a mistake telling Charlie about my other life.

"OK," I said. "The President sent me to the South Pole. To deliver an armored truck full of money to the guys who stole Manhattan. They captured me and tried to feed me to a giant python. Only I broke out of my chains and tied the python into a huge knot."

"That is so awesome!" said Charlie.

Charlie's about the only kid I can talk to. I tried talking to other superheroes once, but that was a disappointment. I went to a meeting of the League of Superheroes. That's this club we belong to. They were all there, in costume. Superman. Superboy. Batman and Robin. Captain Marvel and Captain Marvel Jr. Spider-Man. Wonder Woman. The Incredible Hulk. Everybody.

They were all pretty snotty, actually. The adult superheroes stood around, bragging about all the superhero things they did. I didn't really think superheroes were supposed to brag. Also, I didn't find them all that great. Spider-Man had sticky hands.

Superman had super bad breath. The Incredible Hulk kept backing into things and breaking them. And Captain Marvel smelled like he hadn't showered in about a month.

I tried talking to the younger guys — Superboy, Robin, and Captain Marvel Jr. — but they weren't much better. "Holy moly!" said Captain Marvel Jr., "you're just a baby. What are you even *doing* here?"

"Don't talk that way to him," said Wonder Woman. "He's one of us." Captain Marvel Jr. kind of slunk away. I thought Wonder Woman was nice to do that, but then she started gossiping about the other super-heroes and I got bored.

About the only superhero I met there that I liked was Tortoise Man. He was an older guy. He had gray hair, a big bald spot, and his belly was kind of hanging over his belt. Part of his costume was a big, heavy turtle shell that made him move kind of slow. He seemed pretty tired of all the super-hero stuff, but he was nice.

"Being a superhero is a thankless job, son," he said, "and it isn't as glamorous as you might think."

"I don't think it's glamorous at all, sir," I said. "I think it's a pain in the butt."

Tortoise Man laughed.

"Well said, young man. Very well said. Tell me — if it's as thankless and unglam-orous as you say it is, why do you bother to do it?"

"I'm afraid I have no choice, sir," I said. "If somebody's in trouble, I pretty much have to do whatever I can to help them."

Tortoise Man nodded and looked at me

seriously. His eyes looked a little wet.

"You're a good man, Maximum Boy," he said. "If you ever need advice or help, call me. Here's my number." He handed me a card. It read: TORTOISE MAN. SUPERHERO, CHAMPION OF THE WEAK, ENEMY OF EVILDOERS EVERYWHERE, HANDYMAN. NO JOB TOO BIG OR TOO SMALL. BUT NO HEAVY LIFTING, PLEASE. 555-7241.

So, besides Tortoise Man, I stopped trying to make friends with superheroes. I think most of those guys are just in it for the clothes. I think most of their costumes look pretty dorky.

Right about the time recess was over, my beeper went off. I looked at the number on the beeper. It was the White House calling.

CHAPTER 6

A five-star general was in the Oval Office with the President.

"Maximum Boy, I'd like you to meet General Norman Shmegeggi," said the President. "General Shmegeggi, this is Maximum Boy, the brave young man who's been trying to help us save Manhattan."

"We're all proud of you, son," said General Shmegeggi. "The armed forces are solidly behind you. The Army, the Navy, the Air Force, the Marines. We're all behind you."

"In what way are you all behind me, sir?" I asked.

"In the way of watching you on the ten o'clock news and yelling, 'Way to go, Maximum Boy!' " said General Shmegeggi.

"Maximum Boy, Dr. Zirkon called me today," said the President. "He demanded the one trillion dollars again. I told him to take a long walk off a short pier."

"Good one, sir," I said. "What did he say to that?"

"He said that if he doesn't get the trillion, he'll keep Manhattan," said the President. "I don't know what he plans to do with it. He said we have till five P.M. tonight."

"Maximum Boy," said General Shmegeggi. "Manhattan is now somewhere in the middle of the North Atlantic. It's in heavy seas. It's being whipped by terrible storms. The Seventh Fleet is steaming out there to help, but the earliest they can arrive is tomorrow morning."

"We realize you'd have to miss more school," said the President, "but is there anything you can do to help?"

"Like what, sir?" I asked.

"We'd be grateful if you can get out there and stop Zirkon from keeping Manhattan," said General Shmegeggi. "Heck, I'd do it myself, but the rest of my day today is pretty well booked. Meetings, meetings, meetings. If it was tomorrow, it would be a whole other ball game."

"We wouldn't be asking you to miss another day of school if we didn't think this was really important," said the President. "I'll write a note to your teacher."

"Well, sir," I said, "I'll do my best."

"Good boy," said the President. "And if you can do it before five tonight, that would be really neat."

CHAPTER 7

I phoned my mom.

"When are you coming home, Max?" she asked.

"Not just yet, Mom," I said. "The President wants me to do another thing for him first."

"Right now, you mean?"

"Yeah," I said.

"What kind of thing does he want you to do?"

"Well, it's kind of a secret," I said. I thought if I told her any more she might worry.

"Does this have to do with the theft of Manhattan?"

"It might," I said. "But I really can't discuss it, Mom."

"Well, be careful," she said. "Did you have your lunch yet?"

"Not really."

"Well, ask the President if he can fix you something. I don't want you going off on a mission with an empty stomach. It's not healthy."

"OK, Mom."

"Max, when you come back, could you come by way of Milwaukee?"

"Sure. Why?"

"I heard the A&P there is having a big sale on cheese. I'd like you to pick up a gallon of cottage cheese and a twenty-pound wheel of cheddar."

"OK, Mom."

Before I left the White House, the President's personal chef made me lunch. He said I could have anything I wanted. I looked at the menu. It was pretty fancy. There was steak in lobster sauce, lobster in steak sauce, stuff like that. I ordered a peanut butter sandwich and a chocolate milk shake. They served it to me on a big silver tray with a cloth napkin and real silverware.

I finished lunch at one-thirty. Then I flew out to sea to try and find Manhattan. Even though General Shmegeggi had given me a pretty good idea of where it was, I couldn't see it. The ocean was really rough. The waves were forty feet high. The wind was shrieking so loudly, I couldn't hear myself think.

But Manhattan is pretty big, and after a while I spotted it. I flew lower and checked it out. Although they were floating at sea, it was still business as usual in the city. And midtown traffic was about the same as always. I hadn't yet figured out where Zirkon planned to take Manhattan. And I sure couldn't stop him before five o'clock if I didn't find out how he was propelling the island. I looked at my watch. It was almost three.

I had to figure it out soon. But first, I thought I'd better let somebody know I was here. I landed at City Hall and went inside to see the mayor.

"Hello, Your Honor," I said. "I'm Maximum Boy. The President sent me to help you out."

"We don't need any help," said the mayor.

"You don't?"

"Not really," said the mayor. "New York has always been able to solve its own problems."

"How are you solving this one?" I asked.

"Well, we're all sitting tight," he said. "We're all pulling together. People in New York are tough. We don't let things like power blackouts or citynappings bother us."

"I see," I said.

"Everything is business as usual in Manhattan," said the mayor. "Although I admit that floating in the North Atlantic has cut down a little on our tourist business."

I went outside again. I still had no idea where Zirkon planned to take Manhattan. Somehow, I had to figure that out and stop it before five o'clock. I leaped back into the air and started flying back and forth, scanning the island. I turned on my X-ray vision and scanned the city, building by building. I couldn't see a thing.

My X-ray vision did find the motor that drove Manhattan out to sea. It was a nuclear engine with a propeller. Right under the end of the island that used to connect to the Bronx. But that wasn't helping me solve my problem. I kept looking.

It was 4:45 P.M. before I spotted something weird. Manhattan wasn't calmly sailing along anymore. It had started to turn sharply south. Then it started picking up speed. Lots of speed.

And then I realized where Zirkon planned to take Manhattan. To Antarctica! To his hideout at the South Pole!

Now I knew what I had to do. I had to dive underwater and somehow stop those propellers.

I'm embarrassed to tell you this, but with all my superpowers I'm not so great in the water. Oh, I can swim OK. It's just that I don't really like to put my face in the water. The water goes up my nose. When I'm at the beach, I always wear nose clips. Now I was in the middle of the North Atlantic without my nose clips. But I had to find a way to stop those propellers before five P.M.

I jumped into the water. The sea was

freezing cold. There were chunks of ice the size of school buses floating around. One of my powers is being able to heat myself up so I don't freeze in cold water. But that works mostly when I'm in a swimming pool and the temperature is around seventy degrees. It doesn't do much in the North Atlantic with chunks of ice the size of school buses. I took a deep breath, held my nose, and dove underneath the island.

Have you ever seen the underside of an island? It looks really weird. All kinds of stuff is hanging down off it. Roots of trees. Huge pipes. Subway systems. I swam to the end of the island where the propellers were. The island was moving faster now. I could barely swim to keep up with it.

I can hold my breath a pretty long time.

Over a minute. Then I have to come up for another breath. I had to come up twelve times before I saw it. A long silver tube with a gigantic propeller attached. In big black letters it said: NUCLEAR MOTOR.

I swam to the surface and took another gulp of air. Then I dove back underwater. As I reached out to grab the propeller, something grabbed me by the ankle.

I looked down. Two guys in black wet

suits and oxygen tanks were right below me. A tall one and a short one with a duck's bill and webbed feet. Dr. Zirkon and Nobblock! Dr. Zirkon carried a long, pointy speargun!

CHAPTER 8

Nobblock was the one holding my ankle. I could see him grinning up at me through his face mask. Then he grabbed my other ankle, too. Dr. Zirkon swam up and jabbed at me with his speargun. I moved out of the way, but not quite fast enough. The blade of the speargun got me on the shoulder. A little trickle of blood started oozing out of the place where he got me.

I wrenched my ankles away from Nobblock. I grabbed the nuclear motor and yanked hard. It wouldn't come off the island. Then Nobblock got me from behind in a headlock. I'm pretty strong, even underwater. I reached behind my head and grabbed Nobblock by the elbows. Then I flipped him over my head. He looked pretty angry. Water had definitely gone up my nose.

I swam up to the motor and gave the propeller a karate chop with the heel of my hand. It split in two and stopped spinning!

Nobblock attacked again. I dodged him, then caught him in a martial arts hold and slammed him against the bottom of the is-land. In spite of the water in my nose, I was winning. The problem was, these guys were breathing air from oxygen tanks and I wasn't. I had only a few seconds of breath left.

That's when I saw it. A giant octopus. It had dead-looking eyes the size of dinner plates. It had huge, wavy tentacles that had to be six feet long. It had a gigantic parrot-like beak for a mouth. It was swimming right toward us!

My lungs were about to explode. With the last bit of strength in my body, I shot to the surface and hauled myself up onto dry land. Well, not so dry, but land.

I was gulping air so hard I had to lie down for a minute. The island was still moving, but it was going slower and slower. I had stopped the motor! I had saved Manhattan from being citynapped!

I watched the surface of the water. There

was a lot of thrashing around. Then nothing. Neither Dr. Zirkon nor Nobblock appeared. I figured the octopus had finished what I started.

When I told the mayor what happened, he seemed pretty impressed. "You have done the city of New York a very great service, Maximum Boy," he said. "We are grateful to you."

"Thank you, sir," I said. "Now I'm going to try to get you back to New York Harbor."

"By the way," said the mayor, "is that spaghetti sauce on your shoulder?"

"No sir, blood."

"Put a little cornstarch on the stain when you get home," he said.

"Thank you, sir."

"If that doesn't work, Carbona stain remover will take it right out."

"Thank you, sir," I said. "I'll try to remember that."

I swam to the southern end of the island. I placed both hands firmly on the end and began kicking as hard as I could. The island began to move in the direction of the United States. In a few minutes we were whizzing through the ocean so fast, it left a wake as high as the Empire State Building.

The people on board the island realized what I was doing and they began to cheer. I whizzed Manhattan all the way back to New York Harbor. Then I slowly pushed it up to the Bronx and fit it back into place.

The mayor said I didn't have to hang

around and reattach the bridges and tunnels or anything.

"Hey, that's what we have city workers for," he said.

The next morning, the mayor held a ticker tape parade in my honor. Just like they do for baseball teams that win the World Series. He invited my mom and dad and Tiffany, but they had to be in disguise so nobody would find out my true identity. They made Dad dress like Ronald McDonald, Mom like Big Bird, and Tiffany like Barney the dinosaur.

The streets were still wet, and there were dead fish all over the place, but nobody seemed to mind. In fact, everybody cheered their heads off. It felt great.

Then the mayor gave me the key to the

city. I wasn't sure how that worked. What good was a key to the city? Was that in case I came to New York one night and found it locked?

Anyway, my family was pretty proud. After the parade, the President said he'd fly us all back to Chicago on *Air Force One*. Tiffany was so happy she almost got over having to dress like Barney the dinosaur. Then a terrible thing happened.

"Folks," said the President, "I'm afraid I have some disappointing news. *Air Force One* is temporarily out of service. The stabilizer isn't working, and the darn rearview mirror just fell off. I'm afraid you're going to have to fly back to Chicago on a regular civilian airliner."

Mom and Dad looked disappointed, but Tiffany burst into tears.

I felt really bad to see them so unhappy. I took the President aside.

"Sir," I said to him. "My family was really counting on flying in *Air Force One*. If the plane can't fly, then maybe I could put them in it anyway and carry it back to Chicago. Just like I did with the armored truck."

"Sorry, Maximum Boy," said the President. "No can do. *Air Force One* is already being worked on. But if you'd like to borrow another government vehicle, be my guest. You've sure earned it."

"Well," I said, "when I was at the Air and Space Museum a few years ago, I saw a Mercury space capsule. How's about if I carry my family back to Chicago in that?"

The President thought it over and then said it would be fine for me to borrow a Mercury space capsule.

"Just try not to get any more dings in it," he said.

So that's how Mom, Dad, and Tiffany got back to Chicago. In a Mercury space capsule. Of course, I had to fly down to Washington first to get it, but that wasn't a big deal. Then I took them on the long way home, by way of Africa. I flew low over a herd of elephants and a pride of lions. They really got a kick out of that.

I landed the space capsule at O'Hare Airport. Then we took a cab to our apartment. The minute we walked in the door, the phone rang.

It was the President.

"How'd your folks like their ride in the space capsule?" asked the President.

"They liked it a lot, sir," I said.

"Good," said the President. "Max, I'm afraid I have some bad news. I have another case for you, and it's urgent. How soon can you get back to Washington?"

"Is that the President?" whispered my mom.

"Yes, Mom," I whispered. "Sir, what's the new case about?"

"Tell him thanks for the space capsule ride," whispered my mom.

"OK, Mom," I whispered. "Mom says thanks for the space capsule ride. Sir, how soon did you want me back in Washington? Can it wait till after dinner?"

"Only if dinner is a Pop-Tart," said the President. "Max, you are not going to believe what just happened!"

Check out this sneak preview from the next nail-biting Maximum Boy adventure!

THE DAY EVERYTHING TASTED LIKE BROCCOLI

It was already dark by the time I found a warehouse that looked like the one that Tortoise Man and Tortoise Woman described. It was big. And creepy looking. Rusting metal walls. No windows. Surrounded by a hurricane fence topped with rolls of razor wire. Inside I heard the barking of guard dogs.

I leaped over the fence and rang the

doorbell. At first there was no answer. I rang again. The barking of the dogs got louder. Then the huge, heavy door creaked open. It was pretty dark inside, but I could see a guy standing in the doorway. He wore a tuxedo. His hair was shiny and parted in the middle. He had a skinny moustache and a head the size of a watermelon.

The dogs were going crazy. They were barking and baring their teeth.

I growled loudly. They looked startled and backed away.

"May I help you?" asked the guy with the watermelon-sized head.

"Who are you?" I asked.

"The Head Waiter. And what is your name?"

"Maximum Boy. May I come in?"

"Do you have a reservation?"

"A reservation? Uh, no. I'm here to see the Tastemaker."

"I'm sorry. If you have no reservation, you may not come in."

He started to close the door. I held it open with my foot.

He pushed me roughly on the chest. I grabbed his hand and squeezed it so hard I heard something snap inside of it. He gasped at the pain.

"Sorry I had to do that," I said. "After I leave, get an ice pack and put it on that hand for about thirty minutes. And now, let me see the Tastemaker."

"Never!" said the Head Waiter.

"Eet ees all right, Egon," said a voice behind him. It sounded like a French accent, but I wasn't sure.

A man stepped out of the shadows. He

flipped a switch and the entire warehouse was suddenly awfully bright. The man was very tall and very skinny. He was dressed in a white chef's outfit, a tall white chef's hat, and a white mask. He had no hands. Where his hands should be were a steel soup ladle and a meat cleaver.

"I am ze Tastemaker," he said. "To what do I owe ze honor of a visit from ze great Maximum Boy?"

I stepped inside the warehouse. It was an amazing place. It was painted this very bright shiny white color. There were huge stainless steel machines for making food. Giant blenders and mixers and stuff. A wide conveyor belt ran from one corner of the warehouse to the other. Dozens of carving knives and meat cleavers hung on the walls. Baskets of rotting fruit and vegetables covered the floor.

"I'm here to make a citizen's arrest," I said. I grabbed the Tastemaker firmly by the arm.

"Hoho!" said the Tastemaker. "And for wheech crime do you make such an arrest?"

"The crime of making everything in California, Arizona, Nevada, and Oregon taste like steamed broccoli."

The Tastemaker burst out laughing.

"First," he said when he stopped laughing, "I do not make ze food taste like ze steamed broccoli. And even eef I did, thees ees not against ze law."

I grabbed his pinky finger and started bending it backward. The Tastemaker squealed like a little girl.

"Stop eet! Stop eet!" he shrieked.

"If I stop, will you tell me the truth?"

"Yais! Yais! Owww!"

I released his pinky finger.

"Zat really *hurt*," he said. "You deed not have to *hurt* me."

"Tell me the truth or I'll do it again."

"OK, *OK*," he said.

"I'm waiting," I said. "Tell me how you made everything taste like broccoli."

"Seemple," he said. "I eenvent a machine called ze Brain Poacher. Eet tune een on ze frequency of human brain waves. Eet reach ze part of ze people's brains zat affect taste — right next to ze hippocampus — and zen I tune eet to Steamed Broccoli. Do you know what ees ze hippocampus?"

"Sure."

"What ees eet?"

"It's, uh, where hippos go to college."

ABOUT THE AUTHOR

When he was a kid, author Dan Greenburg used to be a lot like Maximum Boy—he lived with his parents and sister in Chicago, he was skinny, he wore glasses and braces, he was a lousy athlete, he was allergic to milk products, and he became dizzy when exposed to math problems. Unlike Maximum Boy, Dan was never able to lift locomotives or fly.

As an adult, Dan has written over 40 books for both kids and grown-ups, which have been reprinted in 23 countries. His kids' books include the series The Zack Files, which is also a TV series. His grown-up books include *How to Be a Jewish Mother* and *How to Make Yourself Miserable*. Dan has written for the movies and TV, the Broadway stage, and most national magazines. He has appeared on network TV as an author and comedian. He is still trying to lift locomotives and fly.